Kylie Jean

Cooking Queen

by Marci Peschke

illustrated by Tuesday Mourning

PICTURE WINDOW BOOKS
a capstone imprint

J PESCHKE
STEP UP

Kylie Jean is published by Picture Window Books
A Capstone Imprint
1710 Roe Crest Drive
North Mankato, Minnesota 56003
www.mycapstone.com

Library of Congress Cataloging-in-Publication Data
Cataloging-in-Publication information is on file with the Library of Congress.
Names: Peschke, Marci, author. | Mourning, Tuesday, illustrator.
Title: Cooking Queen
ISBN 978-1-4795-9899-1 (library binding)
ISBN 978-1-4795-9901-1 (paper over board)
ISBN 978-1-4795-9905-9 (eBook PDF)

$16.99

MAR   '18

Creative Director: *Nathan Gassman*

Graphic Designer: *Sarah Bennett*

Editor: *Shelly Lyons*

Production Specialist: *Laura Manthe*

Design Element Credit:
Shutterstock: blue67design, kosmofish

Printed and bound in the United States of America.
010368F17

For the true cooking queen, KJH, and
two little bakers — Maxie and Gwen
— MP

Table of Contents

All About Me, Kylie Jean!......................7

Chapter One
Picking Pecans.............................. 11

Chapter Two
Potluck Party 24

Chapter Three
Official Entry.............................35

Chapter Four
Filling the Pantry......................46

Chapter Five
Chef Kylie Jean.........................58

Chapter Six
Main-Dish Misery....................................67

Chapter Seven
Good Morning Gourmet 74

Chapter Eight
Bake Off 87

Chapter Nine
We Are THANKFUL 101

All About Me, Kylie Jean!

My name is Kylie Jean Carter. I live in a big, sunny, yellow house on Peachtree Lane in Jacksonville, Texas, with Momma, Daddy, and my two brothers, T.J. and Ugly Brother.

T.J. is my older brother, and Ugly Brother is . . . well . . . he's really a dog. Don't you go telling him he is a dog. Okay? I mean it. He thinks he is a real true person.

He is a black-and-white bulldog. His front looks like his back, all smashed in. His face is all droopy like he's sad, but he's not.

His two front teeth stick out, and his tongue hangs down. (Now you know why his name is Ugly Brother.)

Everyone I love to the moon and back lives in Jacksonville. Nanny, Pa, Granny, Pappy, my aunts, my uncles, and my cousins all live here. I'm extra lucky, because I can see all of them any time I want to!

My momma says I'm pretty. She says I have eyes as blue as the summer sky and a smile as sweet as an angel. (Momma says pretty is as pretty does. That means being nice to the old folks, taking care of little animals, and respecting my momma and daddy.)

But I'm pretty on the outside and on the inside. My hair is long, brown, and curly.

I wear it in a ponytail sometimes, but my absolute most favorite is when Momma pulls it back in a princess style on special days.

I just gave you a little hint about my big dream. Ever since I was a bitty baby I have wanted to be an honest-to-goodness beauty queen. I even know the wave. It's side to side, nice and slow, with a dazzling smile. I practice all the time, because everybody knows beauty queens need to have a perfect wave.

I'm Kylie Jean, and I'm going to be a beauty queen. Just you wait and see!

Chapter One
Picking Pecans

On Saturday morning when Ugly Brother and I wake up, it's cold. It's finally sweatshirt weather! The air in my room is chilly. I snuggle under the covers. Sometimes it takes a long time for fall to come to Texas.

I look over at Ugly Brother. He is snuggled at the end of my bed. "Do you know it's almost Thanksgiving?" I ask.

He barks, "Ruff, ruff."

Two barks — that's a yes! Then again, maybe he's just barking because he heard me say *Thanksgiving*. Ugly Brother loves turkey so much. Drumsticks are his favorite!

"Don't get too excited. It's still three weeks away," I tell him.

Finally, I scoot out of bed. I pull on my jeans and sweatshirt. Ugly Brother barely moves.

"Come on, lazy bones!" I call. "You can't stay in bed all day. Today we're picking pecans so I can make my famous pecan pie for Sunday dinner."

Ugly Brother tucks his face between his paws, looking disappointed. But then the smell of bacon wafts up from the kitchen downstairs. It distracts him. He bolts from the bed and starts to scamper, and I quickly follow.

If we were racing to the breakfast table, Ugly Brother would win. By the time I get to the kitchen, he's standing next to my chair with a piece of  bacon hanging out of his mouth. It looks just like a tongue.

"Someone sure loves bacon!" I say.

Momma turns to look at Ugly Brother, and we both laugh. Then she puts more bacon in the big black skillet. She makes eggs and toast too.

Daddy and T.J. come in, and we all eat breakfast together. Everyone talks about our Saturday plans.

It's a nice brisk fall day, so Momma and I
decide to take Ugly Brother on a walk to Pecan
Park to pick pecans after breakfast. Our route
takes us past our neighbor Miss Clarabelle's house.
We wave as we pass.

Miss Clarabelle waves back from her rocking chair. Her porch is dotted with pumpkins of all shapes and sizes. She even has the big flat round pumpkins that look like Cinderella's carriage. People call them Cinderella pumpkins.

"Isn't Miss Clarabelle's porch pretty?" I say. "I just love her Cinderella pumpkins! They remind me of princesses, and princesses make me think about queens. You know how much I love queens!"

"Those Cinderella pumpkins are so short and squatty," says Momma. "I like the traditional orange ones that didn't get cut for Halloween."

Momma has Ugly Brother on a leash so he won't run away. Momma and I each have a big brown paper sack with handles to hold the pecans we will gather.

We are enjoying the colorful leaves and the beautiful fall day. It's still early as we walk through town. On our way to the park, we see shop owners starting to switch their signs from *closed* to *open.*

When we pass the Harvest Food Pantry, I notice they have a giant sign in the window. It says *Feed a Needy Family for the Holidays.*

"Look, Momma," I say. "What does the sign mean, exactly?"

"We have so many good things to eat, Kylie Jean," says Momma. "Some people are less fortunate, and they go hungry. We should fill a bag at the grocery store to donate to the food pantry."

I nod my head. For the rest of the walk, I'm quiet. I'm thinking that there has to be a way to help lots of hungry families. If I had a lot of money, I'd buy a truck full of groceries for them.

When we get to the park, Momma says, "You're awful quiet, sugar. Are you ready to pick pecans?"

"I'm thinking about something important," I tell her. "Since we're already at the park, I'm going to pick pecans and think at the same time!"

Momma and I decide to have a race to see who can get the most pecans. We spread out under the tall trees and begin to fill our bags. I'm thinking I have an advantage since Momma has to hold the doggie leash and pick up pecans. Plus Ugly Brother keeps trying to get into her bag and eat the pecans!

Momma and I
both laugh at our
silly doggie, because
these nuts are still in
the shell. This year
there's a good pecan
crop, so it's easy to fill
our bags. The nuts in
my bag get closer and
closer to the top.

"I'm done!" Momma calls to me. "My bag is
filled to the brim."

"Yay, Momma!" I shout.

Momma walks over to me. She looks in my bag.
It's almost full. "Yay, Kylie Jean!" she says.

"Well, I think we have enough pecans," I say.

"We sure do!" replies Momma. "Let's head back home, sugar."

Momma tugs on the doggie leash, and we set out for home. Ugly Brother is slow. I think he's tired! Momma and I pass the Harvest Food Pantry again. I'm still working on a plan to get a truck full of food for those hungry folks.

Soon we are back home. Momma preheats the oven for my famous pecan pie. The secret is in my crust. The recipe was my great-grandmother's. Everyone called her Maw.

Momma and I wash our hands and put on our aprons. Together we measure out the ingredients for the crust.

I put the flour in the bowl. Momma adds the shortening. I add a pinch of salt. We use a kitchen tool called a pastry cutter to mix the dough together. We know it's ready when the dough looks like a bowl full of little white peas. The last thing we do is add several tablespoons of ice water. And then we mix it all together with a fork. I gently pat the dough into a ball.

Next, I sprinkle flour on the counter under the ball of dough. I roll out the dough with my wooden rolling pin. Then I use Momma's trick. Very carefully, I roll the circle of dough over the edge of the rolling pin. Then I move the dough into the pie pan. Momma cuts off the extra dough, and I crimp the edges with a fork.

"You are quite the baker, little lady," says Momma. "Now let's make the filling."

"Yes, ma'am," I reply. "Can we put the leftover dough on a pan with some cinnamon sugar too?"

"Of course!" Momma tells me.

We make the filling by placing corn syrup and butter into the mixing bowl. Then we add sugar, eggs, salt, and vanilla. Once it's all mixed, we add the pecans. Momma pours the filling into the crust. Then she pops it into the oven.

When the pie is finished baking, we put it on the table to cool. A mouth-watering, brown sugary, caramel perfume fills the air.

Daddy says, "I'm ready for some of that delicious pie!"

T.J. says, "Me too!"

"No one is eating any of this pie," Momma says. "It's for the potluck at Nanny's house tomorrow."

Potluck dinners are the best because everyone brings a dish to share. Usually Nanny makes Sunday dinner. But Momma and Aunt Susie think it might be nice to give her a break. Plus, my cousin Lucy will be there tomorrow. I can't wait to see her!

Maw's Pie Crust

Ingredients

- 2 ¼ cups all-purpose flour
- ⅓ cup butter-flavored shortening
- ⅓ cup regular shortening
- 5–8 tablespoons of ice cold water
- pinch of salt

Instructions

1. Chill shortening for 30 minutes.
2. Stir flour and salt together in a deep bowl. Using a pastry blender, cut the shortening into the flour until the dry ingredients form pea-sized crumbs.
3. Using a fork, stir in 1 tablespoon of ice water at a time until a dough ball forms.
4. Roll out on a floured surface. Put dough in pie pan. Trim and crimp edges. Now you are ready for pie filling!

Chapter Two
Potluck Party

On Sunday morning before church, Momma and I make French toast for breakfast.

"You are really enjoying cooking this weekend," says Momma.

"I like to cook all the time!" I tell her.

I crack the eggs with a *tap, tap, tap* on the edge of the bowl. Then I pour in the milk. Next, I swirl in the vanilla and sugar. Finally, I add a dash of cinnamon. I use a metal whisk to stir the mixture.

"Momma, are you going to help me dip the bread in the egg mixture and flip it onto the skillet?" I ask.

She replies, "I will if you find T.J. and Daddy to set the table."

"You've got a deal!" I say.

T.J. comes in just in time to put the plates on the table. He's tall, so it's easier for him to get them out of the cupboard anyway.

Daddy comes in last. He passes the skillet to T.J. to place on the table. Then he grabs a small piece and stuffs it into his mouth. He smiles and winks at Momma.

"My compliments to the chef," Daddy says. "This breakfast is delicious!"

"Kylie Jean is the chef this morning! And you should wait until you get to the table to eat your food," Momma tells him.

Daddy winks at me.

T.J. nudges Daddy. "Hey, I put the plates on the table," he says.

"Great!" replies Daddy. "And next weekend you and I can cook breakfast."

Momma smiles, and we all start eating our breakfast. Soon Momma looks up at the kitchen clock, and then she jumps up out of her chair.

"Oh, no! We're going to be late for church!" she cries as she grabs her purse.

We all jump up and run around. Daddy grabs the keys. T.J. grabs his jacket. I run for the door.

I almost forget the pie for the potluck dinner at Nanny's house. We're going there straight from church. But thankfully Ugly Brother reminds me by barking in the kitchen.

* * *

Later at Nanny's, the table is piled high with food. There's fried chicken, veggies, desserts, and my special pecan pie too. We all get plates and form a line to dish up. The kids get to go first, then grown-ups, and finally Nanny and Pa. They are the hosts, so they get their plates last. Nanny says it's just good manners to let your guests go first.

When everyone has a plate, Pa says the blessing. Then we all dig in! At first, it's so quiet you could hear a pin drop. Momma says if people aren't talking, it means the food is really tasty.

My best cousin Lucy is sitting right beside me. She leans in toward me. "I don't like to bake much," she whispers, "but I know you do. Your pie is delicious!"

"Cooking is one of my favorite things," I tell her. "Actually, I love cooking almost as much as I love queens and the color pink."

Lucy gasps. "Well, I can't believe it!" she replies. "I thought you'd never love anything as much as you love pink!"

"Momma won all sorts of cooking ribbons at the county fair. I guess she just passed that love of cooking on to me," I explain.

Lucy nods. When we are done, we take our plates to the kitchen. Then we ask if we can go play outside.

Nanny says, "Just for a while. Today, the grandkids wash all of the dishes."

Last weekend, the kids washed them. By the kids, I mean Momma, Daddy, and all the aunts and uncles. It's funny to think of them actually being kids!

On our way to the barn, Lucy and I see most of the grown-ups settled into the den. They're watching the Cowboys play. Daddy says Sunday afternoon football watching should be a requirement.

Lucy and I play tag. I'm only *it* once, but Lucy gets tagged several times. I would say Lucy is a slow runner, but I know she's not.

"Lucy, are you trying to get caught?" I ask her.

Lucy laughs. "Maybe . . . I like being *it* and chasing you around. Then I don't have to worry about getting tagged."

Just then, Nanny calls us in to do the dishes. Momma and Aunt Susie are in the kitchen with Lilly and T.J. Everyone is raving about my pie. Lucy and I get dish towels. We are always part of the dish-drying crew.

I see Momma and Aunt Susie talking quietly in the corner. I think they're up to something because Momma looks a little sick, like she just swallowed a June bug.

She asks Nanny, "Mom, can we have Thanksgiving at my house this year?"

We all look at Nanny and wait for her answer. Now Nanny is the one who looks like she swallowed a June bug!

"It's just that the family has gotten so big, and hosting Thanksgiving dinner will be a lot of work for you," Momma adds.

Nanny asks, "Shelley, are you sure you want to take on this big holiday meal?"

"I am!" says Momma.

Nanny finally nods. "Well, if you're sure, I guess we can try it this year." She seems a little sad. I think she likes cooking for a big bunch.

Aunt Susie is still going on and on about my yummy pie. "Did you hear about that cooking contest for kids on the *Good Morning, Texas* TV show?" she asks.

"No, ma'am," I tell her.

"Shelley, you just have to help Kylie Jean enter that contest," Aunt Susie says.

Momma says, "Kylie Jean can cook a lot of different dishes. I'll check into that contest."

On the way home, Momma and I have a little chat. "Momma, do really think I could enter that cooking contest and be a cooking queen?" I ask. "It sounds fun!"

"Of course you could," says Momma.

"Will you help me enter?" I ask her.

"Sure, sugar!" she says. "I bet we can find out by looking on the Internet. We'll do it this week."

I found out two exciting things today. First, I found out we are having Thanksgiving at our house this year. Second, I'm going to try and enter that cooking contest. I hope there's a prize! Maybe I can use it to buy food for the Harvest Food Pantry.

Cinnamon French Toast
Serves 4

Ingredients

- 1 egg
- 1 teaspoon vanilla
- ½ teaspoon cinnamon
- ¼ cup buttermilk
- 1 tablespoon light brown sugar
- 4 slices bread

Instructions

1. Beat egg, vanilla, brown sugar, and cinnamon in shallow dish. Stir in milk.
2. Dip bread in egg mixture, turning to coat both sides evenly.
3. Cook bread slices on lightly greased nonstick griddle or skillet on medium heat until browned on both sides.
4. Dust with powdered sugar or serve with maple syrup.

Chapter Three
Official Entry

The following night, Momma helps me look up the contest on the Internet. The website says kids who want to enter need to make a video entry. So Tuesday evening, I try to pick out an apron to wear for my video entry for the *Good Morning, Texas* Kids Cooking Contest. Momma laid out several aprons on my bed, and Ugly Brother wants to help me too.

"I need this apron to show the TV station that I am a real true kid chef! If I win, I will be able to do something very important," I tell Ugly Brother.

"I'll be able to help the Harvest Food Pantry!"
I twirl around, showing him my pink cupcake
apron. "Do you like this one?"

Ugly Brother barks, "Ruff." That means no.

I guess he isn't a fan of pink cupcake aprons. Too bad I love pink!

"I bet you'd like a bacon apron!" I joke.

He barks excitedly, "Ruff, ruff! Ruff, ruff!" Then he chases his tail in a circle.

I study all my options. The apron I wear for the contest needs to be special. For a while, I consider Momma's lucky blue-and-white checked apron. I even try it on. She has worn it to every state fair cooking competition, and she always wins.

"I really want to be picked for the contest because I'm good at cooking, not because I'm wearing Momma's lucky apron," I tell him. "Do you know what I mean, Ugly Brother?"

"Ruff, ruff," he barks.

I decide to stick with my pink cupcake apron instead. I run downstairs to show Momma.

"That one is perfect, sugar," Momma says.

Just then, T.J. comes in the back door. He has agreed to help me make my audition video. "Ready to make a movie, Lil' Bit?" he asks.

I nod. Ugly Brother moves close to me so I won't feel nervous. Momma told me that a friendly face will make filming easier. Every time I get nervous, I'm going to think of Ugly Brother with that piece of bacon hanging out of his mouth!

"My video has to have two parts," I tell T.J. "I have to say how long I've been cooking and why I think I should win. Then I have to cook a main dish. I'm making my special pizza. It's one of the only main dishes I know how to make."

"Okay," says T.J. "Let's get started!"

"Can we do the cooking part first?" I ask.

"Sure!" he replies as he picks up his phone to start filming.

While T.J. films me in the kitchen, I get all my ingredients and place them on a cookie sheet. I learned from Momma that a neat kitchen helps a chef make a good dish. I will use crescent rolls for my dough. They're easy peasy! I preheat my oven, and then I press the rolls out in one big piece on a baking sheet.

My nerves still have me feeling a little jumpy inside, but then I see Momma and Ugly Brother watching me. I think about his bacon tongue, and I want to laugh out loud!

Next, I mix softened cream cheese, sour cream, and herbs in a small bowl. When I hear the oven beep, I know it's time to put the crust in and set the timer.

"I'll help you with that, sugar," Momma says as she places the crust in the oven.

"Thanks, Momma," I say.

Next, it's time to slice the vegetables with my tiny chef's knife. Momma watches me closely. She has taught me how to use a knife the proper way.

First, I put the onions in cold water. Then I carefully cut them into rings. Momma taught me that special trick so my eyes won't tear up. Next I slice the mushrooms.

Finally, it's time for the peppers. I have a special plan for them. I'm going to julienne them! That means I'll cut them into thin, shiny green ribbons that are all the same size. This trick should make the TV folks really happy. I hope they'll think I have super chef skills!

The oven timer goes off, and Momma pulls out the crust I made. "Wow, look at that gorgeous golden color!" she says.

Now that the crust is cooked, I spread on the cream cheese topping, making a creamy sauce. Then I add the veggies. The pizza looks beautiful!

T.J. looks impressed. He pauses the video to say, "That looks amazing, Lil' Bit!"

I smile and hold the pizza up so he can get a good shot. Then I begin talking to the camera. "Hey, y'all! I've been cooking for as long as I can remember," I say. "I started out with my pink play kitchen when I was an itty-bitty baby! I think I should win because I am creative, and I put a lot of love into my cooking."

Momma smiles and gives me a thumbs-up.

I continue my speech. "Now, I just bet you thought I was going to make a regular pizza, but I didn't! Using the freshest ingredients is very important to me. I spend a lot of time on a farm. And we get a lot of farm-fresh food to cook up and serve on our table. Fresh food tastes delicious! I sure wish y'all could try this — it's so good!"

Ugly Brother is drooling at my feet. I know because I feel a puddle forming there, but I don't let it distract me!

I smile and take a big bite of pizza. "Yummy!" I exclaim.

"Cut!" says T.J.

"You were perfect, sugar!" says Momma.

"Thanks, Momma," I reply.

Momma and T.J. both step in for a piece of my pizza. I even sneak Ugly Brother a little piece while we watch the finished video. We all agree it turned out pretty good.

Later that day, I cross my fingers as I e-mail my cooking video with help from Momma. Now I have to wait to hear if I am chosen for the contest!

Easy Veggie Pizza Pie
Serves 8

Ingredients

- 2 8-oz. cans refrigerated
- crescent dinner rolls
- ½ cup sour cream
- 8 oz. cream cheese
- 1 tablespoon herb seasoning
- ½ cup each green bell pepper, mushrooms, and red onion

Instructions:

1. Heat oven to 375°F.

2. Unroll both cans of crescent roll dough; separate dough into 4 long rectangles. In an ungreased 15 x 10 x 1-inch pan, press into bottom and up sides to form crust.

3. Bake 13–17 minutes or until golden brown. Cool completely, about 30 minutes.

4. In a small bowl, mix cream cheese, sour cream, and herbs until smooth. Spread over crust. Top with vegetables. Serve immediately.

Chapter Four
Filling the Pantry

On Thursday after school, Momma and I go to the grocery store. I have a grocery list for my busy baking weekend. But I also have a secret mission.

"How was school?" Momma asks as we drive.

"Fine," I reply. "Lucy and I got to work on a science experiment together."

"That sounds exciting," she says.

I shrug.

"Are you feeling okay, sugar?" asks Momma.

"Yes, ma'am," I reply.

When we get to the Piggly Wiggly, they have a poster in the window that says *Harvest Food Pantry: Feed a Hungry Family for the Holidays*. I guess the Piggy Wiggly already knew all about my secret mission!

Inside, I get one of those little shopping carts for kids. Momma gets a big cart, and we start down the first aisle. Momma loads up on canned veggies. I do the same!

Momma looks surprised. "What kind of dessert has green beans in it?" she asks.

"Remember when we went to pick pecans? You said we could fill a bag for the food pantry the next time we went to the store," I remind her.

"I've had a lot on my mind, but yes, I do remember now," Momma replies. "I'm so glad you reminded me!"

Momma helps me pick out corn bread mix, cans of pumpkin, and cranberry sauce. We also grab other food staples like flour, sugar, and shortening. Soon my tiny cart is overflowing!

Momma laughs. "I think we have more than one bag of groceries in your cart," she says.

"Can we drop them off at the pantry on our way home?" I ask.

"Sure, sugar," Momma replies.

We finish shopping and check out.

"We're getting food for the food pantry," I tell the cashier.

"That's wonderful," she says. "I'm proud of you for wanting to help. In fact, I think I may buy some food for the food pantry too. You have inspired me!"

I smile a big smile. That makes me feel really good! "Thanks," I tell her. "I'm happy to help."

Momma and I grab our bags and head to the parking lot. We load up the back of the van with our bags. Then we head downtown to drop off our food at the pantry.

Momma parks the van. "We'll have to drop these bags and go. We have our own groceries in the van too," she says.

"Okay, Momma," I reply.

We pick up the bags of food for donation from the back of the van and walk inside. The pantry is bright and cheerful. The walls are painted a soft yellow. Shelves filled with food items line the walls. But some of the shelves are empty. Just then, I see my neighbor Miss Clarabelle!

"Miss Clarabelle!" I shout. "Are you giving food to the pantry too?"

"Not today, dear," she says. "Today is my day to volunteer here at the pantry."

"What does a volunteer do?" I ask.

"Well, I stock the shelves, and I help families fill their sacks," she tells us. "But sometimes the shelves don't have enough food. That means we have to turn hungry families away."

"I see some empty shelves," I say. "It looks like the pantry needs more food!"

Miss Clarabelle nods as she unpacks our grocery bags. When she's done, she smiles and gives me a big squeezy hug.

"Thank you!" she says. "You've done a great job shopping, Kylie Jean. We hardly ever have cans of pumpkin here. The families will really enjoy some of these special Thanksgiving treats."

"I've got a plan to get more food too," I tell her. "Just you wait and see . . . "

Later that evening, Nanny comes over. She has something covered in clear plastic wrap in her arms. She hands it to Momma, who carefully unwraps it. Inside is the giant family turkey platter.

"I guess it's time for the next generation to take over cooking for the holidays," Nanny says. "So I am passing the platter to you, Shelley."

"Thanks, Mom. I hope I will do a good job feeding the family for Thanksgiving," replies Momma.

Momma and Nanny sit at the kitchen table talking about favorite family recipes. Nanny still looks a little sad. T.J. doesn't notice because Nanny has loaded the platter with her famous butterscotch oatmeal cookies. Momma doesn't seem to notice either. She's busy asking Nanny questions.

"Will all of the family members who live in Jacksonville make it for Thanksgiving this year?" Momma asks Nanny.

"Yes, it will be a very large group this year!" replies Nanny.

Momma turns toward me. "Kylie Jean, can you please get a pen and my notepad from my desk?"

"Yes, ma'am," I reply. I run upstairs and grab Momma's notebook and pen. Then I quickly head back down to the kitchen. I want to help Momma with the Thanksgiving meal.

"Thanks, sugar," Momma says.

"You're welcome," I tell her. "Can I help?"

"Of course," she says.

Nanny smiles and pats the chair next to her. I slide into it. Together, Momma, Nanny, and I make a list of everyone who will be coming to our Thanksgiving feast.

Guest List for Turkey Day

Aunt Susie and family–5
Nanny and Pa–2
Granny and Pappy–2
Louisiana cousins–5
Arkansas cousins–3
Miss Clarabelle–1
Our family–4

That makes a total of 22 guests! And Nanny keeps on thinking of other things that Momma needs to do.

Nanny looks over at T.J. He's still huddled near the turkey tray. "T.J., slow down, or there won't be any cookies left for anyone else," she tells him.

T.J. frowns and sets down a cookie.

"I'm going to be testing out recipes all weekend for the contest," I tell Nanny. "I'm making trail mix, double chocolate crispy rice treats, and chocolate cupcakes with caramel filling and fudge frosting. I promise to bring something extra tasty to Sunday dinner!"

"It's going to be a double-chocolate weekend!" replies Nanny. "Well, it's getting late, so I'll be heading home. I'm looking forward to seeing which of those delicious treats you're going to bring to Sunday dinner!"

Before she leaves, Nanny passes out hugs and kisses to everyone. Then Momma says it's time to do homework and get ready for bed.

Butterscotch Oatmeal Cookies
Makes 24 cookies

Ingredients

- 1 stick softened butter (½ cup)
- 1 cup dark brown sugar
- 1 egg
- ½ teaspoon vanilla
- 1 teaspoon baking powder
- ½ teaspoon cinnamon (optional)

- ½ teaspoon kosher salt
- 1 cup all-purpose flour plus an additional 2 tablespoons
- 1 cup butterscotch chips
- 1 ½ cups rolled oats

Instructions

1. Preheat oven to 350ºF.
2. In a large bowl with a hand mixer or the bowl of a stand mixer, cream together the butter and brown sugar.
3. Add the egg and mix until incorporated. Add the vanilla, baking powder, and salt. Mix until incorporated.
4. Stir in the flour, then stir in the butterscotch chips and rolled oats just until combined. Mixing too much will create tough and dry cookies.
5. Drop rounded mounds of dough (about 2 tablespoons each) onto ungreased cookie sheets. Press down dough mounds slightly with the back of a large spoon before baking.
6. Bake until just lightly browned on the edges and the middle still looks undercooked, about 9 minutes.

Chapter Five
Chef Kylie Jean

Over the weekend, I impressed my family with some super-chocolatey cupcakes! All day Monday at school, though, I can't stop thinking about the *Good Morning, Texas* cooking contest. I just can't wait to find out if the judges liked my video!

When I get home, Momma has something exciting to show me. I have mail! I drop my backpack and run to the box on the kitchen table. It's a very special package from KTRE, the local TV station.

"Momma, this is it!" I shout.

"I've been waiting all day!" Momma cries. "Hurry and open it!"

I rip the brown paper from the box. Ugly Brother helps. I pull the flap open. The box is filled with tissue paper and colorful confetti!

"This is so exciting!" I gush.

I dig through the confetti. The box seems empty, so I hold it up and shake it. A white envelope falls to the floor from its hiding place in the box. Ugly Brother brings it to me and lays it at my feet. It's a letter with the competition rules.

"Come sit at the table and we'll read the letter together," says Momma.

We both pull up a chair. Excitedly, I read the letter out loud.

Dear Kid Chef Contestant,

You made it! We loved your video entry, and we want you to compete in the *Good Morning, Texas* Kids Cooking Contest. Congratulations!

Rules:
There will be three rounds at our studio: snack, main dish, and dessert. A fully-stocked pantry will be provided.

Each kid chef may bring only an adult sous chef to the studio.

Judges will be TV host Joe Conrad, culinary professor Kathy Lane, and local chef and restaurant owner Amy Roberts.

Kid chefs should report to the KTRE studio on Saturday, November 19th for preliminary rounds. The final round will be on live TV at the studio Monday, November 21st. Again, congratulations and good luck!

The winning kid chef will receive a $100 check.

Sincerely,
Amber Jones, Producer

Momma says, "I've been to Amy Roberts' restaurant, Amy's Bistro, and the food is really delicious."

"Can we go there before the contest?" I ask.

"Let's go tonight to celebrate!" Momma says.

"Yay!" I cry.

Ugly Brother barks and runs around the kitchen. He thinks he's going too!

"No dogs allowed at the bistro," says Momma.

Ugly Brother whines. I know he's sad.

"Don't worry," I tell him, "I'll bring you my leftovers in a doggie bag.

I run upstairs to change clothes. I put on a pink dress with a little sparkly sweater. I brush my hair and put a big pink bow in it. While I'm changing, Daddy and T.J. come home. Momma tells them the plan. By the time I get back downstairs, everyone is ready to go.

The bistro is right downtown. On the big glass windows, it says *Amy's Bistro* in fancy black letters. Daddy holds the door open for us.

Inside, the tables have white tablecloths and cloth napkins. Chandeliers twinkle above us, and candles glow on the tables.

"This bistro is so fancy," I exclaim. "I love it!"

Momma says, "Just wait until you taste the food. It's delicious!"

"I'm ready to eat anytime," replies T.J.

We all laugh. The hostess leads us to a table and gives each of us a menu. Our server comes right over to fill our crystal glasses with ice water.

"Should we order a starter?" Daddy asks.

"Let's try the bruschetta," Momma tells him.

Momma has made bruschetta at home before. It's like toast, but it has tomatoes and fresh basil on top. It's delicious!

Everyone is looking over the menu.

T.J. says, "I'm having the steak."

"Me too," says Daddy.

"I'm having something fancy — chicken cordon bleu," I tell them.

"Me too!" Momma says.

Our server takes our order. Before long, the starter is served. Everyone agrees it is delicious!

"Will we see Amy Roberts tonight?" I ask.

"Let's ask our server if she is here," says Daddy.

When the server brings the main dishes, Daddy asks if Chef Amy is cooking tonight. But the server tells us Chef Amy is away at a special event. Her sous chef is cooking tonight instead.

Everyone digs in. My chicken tastes amazing!
It has ham and cheese stuffed inside.

Eating such a tasty main dish reminds me that
I have a problem. I need to make a main dish
other than my pizza to win the contest and become
a cooking queen. I really want to win the one-
hundred-dollar prize. I know that money could buy
a lot of food for hungry families.

I'm not very good at cooking main dishes, but
I know just who to call for help!

Tomato Basil Bruschetta
Serves 6–10

Ingredients

- 1 loaf French bread, sliced
- 6 cherry tomatoes, diced
- 8 fresh basil leaves, cut into ribbons
- 2 tablespoons of Italian dressing
- ¼ cup of extra virgin olive oil
- salt and pepper to taste

Instructions

1. Preheat oven to 450°F.
2. Dice the tomatoes, then mix with dressing.
3. Wash and cut basil into narrow ribbons.
4. Brush sliced bread with olive oil. Bake on a foil-wrapped cookie sheet for 5–7 minutes.
5. Top warm toast with tomato mixture and basil.

Chapter Six
Main-Dish Misery

On Tuesday afternoon, in the middle of our messy kitchen, I ask if I can call Nanny. I really need her help with my main dish. Nanny is an amazing cook.

Momma says, "Yes, you can call Nanny. I'm sorry, but I am way too busy practicing new Thanksgiving recipes to help you!"

"Do you want me to stay here and help you, Momma?" I ask.

"No," she replies. "My plan is to try out these vegetable casseroles so I'll know if they'll work for Thanksgiving Day."

I call Nanny right away. *Ring . . . ring . . . ring!*

Nanny answers, "Lickskillet Farm . . . hello?"

"Hi, Nanny," I say. "It's Kylie Jean. I really need your help! Are you busy this afternoon?"

Nanny is not busy. She is very excited and heads right over to pick me up. On the way to the farm, I look over at Nanny.

"What is it, sugar?" asks Nanny.

"Nanny, will you please be my sous chef for the cooking contest this Saturday?" I ask.

"Yes, yes, yes!" she replies. "Being on your team would make me so happy and excited!"

At Lickskillet Farm, Nanny's kitchen is neat as a pin compared to Momma's. Before we start cooking, I put on my pink cupcake apron. Nanny puts on her checkered apron. Then she places some steak, chicken, and eggs on the kitchen counter.

"What kind of main dish can you make with steak?" Nanny asks.

I think for a few minutes, and then I reply, "How about grilled steak?"

"That's a great idea," Nanny agrees. "But to turn it into a winning idea, you will need to make your main dish extra special."

I see her point. Grilled steak is just steak.

"How about steak tacos?" says Nanny.

"That's a great idea!" I tell her. "Momma has been teaching me how to cook on a grill pan."

First, Nanny and I very carefully slice the steak into thin strips. Then we use a grill pan to cook the strips. We decide to add some other ingredients to our tacos too — sweet potatoes and fresh spinach.

"Nanny, what about the cheese?" I ask.

"How about Brie cheese? And let's use pesto for a sauce," says Nanny.

Pesto is made with olive oil and herbs or nuts. We make ours from pine nuts and basil from Nanny's garden. We crush it all up in the blender.

Next, we cook the chopped sweet potato in a skillet with a little olive oil. When it's almost soft, we add the spinach. The last thing I do is heat whole-wheat tortillas on a griddle.

After stuffing the tortillas and adding the cheese, we taste them.

"These tacos are super yummy!" I say. "I'm going to call them Farmhouse Tacos because the ingredients are fresh from your farm!"

"I love these tacos, and I love you!" says Nanny. She gives me a big squeezy hug.

Just then, I hear Daddy's truck bumping down the dirt road.

"I love you too, Nanny!" I say. "Thanks for making me a main-dish superstar. Goodbye until Saturday!"

I blow her a kiss and head out the back door.

Farmhouse Steak Tacos

Ingredients

- 8 whole-wheat tortillas
- ½ pound skirt steak
- 4 oz. Brie cheese
- ½ bag rinsed fresh spinach
- 2 medium sweet potatoes
- 2 tablespoons olive oil
- ¼ cup pine nuts
- 1 small jar pesto (or make your own)
- salt and pepper

Instructions

1. Brush grill pan lightly with oil. Then place the pan on stovetop set to medium heat. Slice steak and add salt and pepper to taste. Cook until fully browned.

2. Dice sweet potato and cook in skillet with a tablespoon of oil. When almost cooked, stir in ½ bag of spinach.

3. Heat tortillas.

4. Assemble tacos by adding pesto, meat, sweet potato/spinach mix, and cheese. Top with pine nuts.

Chapter Seven
Good Morning Gourmet

On Saturday morning, I wake up when it's still as dark as the inside of a pocket. I don't want to be late! Ugly Brother is a big sleepyhead. He doesn't want to get up, but he watches me get ready. I put on my pink T-shirt and black pants.

Downstairs, Momma is also up early. She's waiting to braid my hair. I sit down in front of her, and she gives me some advice as she braids.

"If you get nervous, all you have to do is think of Ugly Brother cheering you on," she tells me. "Remember, Nanny will be there to help you as your sous chef. In fact, Nanny will be here any minute to pick you up. I wish I could go with you, but you can only take your sous chef. You've got this, Kylie Jean!"

"I really want to win, so I'll do my best!" I reply.

"Maybe this will help," Momma says. She holds up a pink ribbon with sparkly cupcakes on it. The ribbon looks just like my special apron!

"Momma, that's beautiful!" I cry. "Thanks so much."

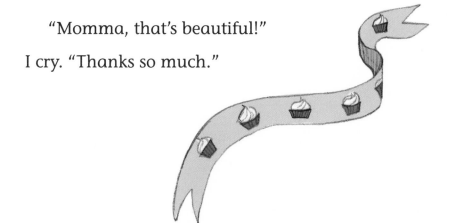

Momma ties the ribbon in my hair. "I have one for Nanny too," she says as she hands me a checkered headband.

"Nanny will love this," I tell her. "I'm going to surprise her with it!" I grab my pink cupcake apron and tuck the headband into a pocket.

Momma hands me a muffin and a glass of milk. I gobble up the muffin and chug down the milk. I finish just as Nanny arrives at the door.

"Ready?" she asks.

"Yup!" I shout.

Momma says, "Whoa, wait a minute! I want to give you a good-luck hug!"

She gives me a big squeezy hug. Nanny and I head out to the car and drive to the TV station.

Inside the studio, we have to sign in. We go straight to the desk in the lobby. A nice woman with *Mabel* on her name badge hands us a clipboard. At the top it says *Good Morning, Texas Kids Cooking Contest Contestants.* Down the side, it lists the names of all the kids and their sous chefs.

Once we're signed in, I put on my apron and tie it tight. Nanny puts hers on too.

"Nanny, I have a surprise for you," I tell her. "You can wear this too." I hand her the blue-and-white checkered headband.

"This is perfect!" says Nanny as she ties the headband around her head. "Thank you."

"Okay, then," says Mabel. "I'll just take you back to the studio."

We walk through a building bigger than my school. Mabel says there are a lot of sets at the station. There are some for morning programs, some for news, and some for specials.

The set for the morning show has been converted into a large kitchen. It has ten miniature cooking stations. Each one has a cooktop, an oven, and a small workspace. Each station also has a stool. I'm glad because I'm a bit too short to reach the cooking area. There is also a huge refrigerator and pantry area to use.

Mabel introduces us to Amber Jones, the producer.

"Nice to meet you, Miss Jones," I say.

"Just call me Amber," she replies. "Welcome to the set. There will be nine other kids from ages eight to twelve competing with you today."

Guess what? One of the other kids competing, whose name is Colton, says his dad is a real chef. He's also Colton's sous chef. I'm not worried, though. Nanny is a fantastic cook, and I have her!

It's time for round one. All of us kid chefs head to our stations with our sous chefs. Amber reads the rules out loud. I'm so excited, I feel as jumpy as a kernel of corn in a popcorn popper! We have just forty-five minutes to make a snack. I take a deep breath.

Amber counts down, "Ten, nine, eight, seven, six, five, four, three, two, one . . . the clock starts now!"

All the kid chefs and their assistants start running around like crazy! I grab a cookie sheet to hold all our ingredients.

"Great idea!" Nanny says.

"I learned this trick from Momma," I tell her.

Next, I grab oats, pumpkin seeds, maple syrup, pecans, and raisins. Then I get brown sugar, salt, dried cranberries, and white chocolate chips. I send Nanny to the refrigerator to get butter. My plan is to make a fall trail mix. I think the judges might enjoy the flavors.

Nanny preheats the oven while I put the pecans on a cookie sheet to toast them. Nanny waits for my signal to put them in. Finally, I hear the buzz that tells me the oven is preheated. I give Nanny the thumbs-up. She puts the pecans in, and I ask her to melt the butter in the microwave.

Next, I carefully measure out all of the dry ingredients into a bowl. I have memorized my recipe, which is good because I will only have a few minutes to mix my snack. We will need time to bake it in the oven.

Nanny comes back with the melted butter, and I stir it together with the salt, brown sugar, and maple syrup. Suddenly, I realize the pecans are still in the oven.

"Nanny, the pecans!" I shout.

Nanny runs over and pulls the pan out of the oven. "We got them out just in time!" she says.

The girl next to me named Gwen says, "I'm glad your pecans are okay. If they had burned, that would have been an awful setback."

"Me too! Thanks!" I reply.

I stir everything together and spread the pecans back out on the baking sheet. Nanny puts the pan back in the oven. When it is done and slightly cooled, we add white chocolate chips. We finish right before Amber calls time.

The judges for today are Amber and the camera crew. They try all the snacks. Some kids have made a meal, not a snack. Gwen put too much salt in her cheesy tater tots. I'm sad that she's out. She seemed so nice.

I'm nervous, but I want to jump for joy when Amber calls out the names of the kid chefs moving on to the next round. The five kids who are going to make a main dish are Colton, Maxie, Jake, Ashley, and me! For the next round, the main dish, we will have forty-five minutes.

When Amber calls time to start, I go straight for the steak. I ask Nanny to get the grill pan while I gather the rest of the ingredients. We both stay focused and cook, and our Farmhouse Steak Tacos turn out great!

Everyone presents his or her main dish. Colton has made a very delicious-looking pot of stew. I see Maxie's plate, and it looks beautiful. Ashley and Jake have made dishes that look really good too. How will the judges pick the finalists?

I see the judges taste all of the dishes, and they keep talking and looking at their clipboard notes. Then they taste my tacos and Colton's stew a second time. I'm so nervous! I try to think of Ugly Brother cheering me on.

Finally Amber says, "The two kid chefs cooking on live TV on Monday will be Kylie Jean Carter and Colton Brooks. Congratulations!"

Nanny and I jump up and down excitedly!

"We did it, we did it!" I cheer.

Nanny says, "Let's call your momma and tell her the good news!"

Now we have to wait until Monday for the final competition. Colton will have his dad for his sous chef again, but I will have Nanny! I give her a big squeezy hug.

"You're my secret good luck charm, Nanny!" I tell her.

Nanny smiles all the way home.

Pumpkin Trail Mix

Ingredients

- 3 cups rolled oats
- 1 cup dried cranberries
- ½ cup raisins
- ½ cup pumpkin seeds
- ½ cup pure maple syrup

- ½ cup toasted pecans
- ¼ cup brown sugar
- ¼ cup butter, melted
- ½ teaspoon salt
- 1 cup white chocolate chips

Instructions

1. Preheat oven to 300°F.

2. In a large bowl, stir to combine rolled oats, dried cranberries, and pumpkin seeds.

3. On a cookie sheet, toast pecans in oven for 3–5 minutes until they are shiny but not burned. Add to bowl of dry ingredients.

4. In a separate bowl, stir to combine maple syrup, brown sugar, melted butter, and salt. Pour wet ingredients over the oats and mix well.

5. Pour the trail mix onto a rimmed sheet pan and spread it out evenly with a spatula. Bake for 30 minutes, stirring halfway through the baking process.

6. Let the trail mix cool completely, and then add white chocolate chips. Store in an airtight container at room temperature for up to two weeks.

Chapter Eight
Bake Off

On Monday, Nanny and I need to head back to the KTRE studio bright and early in the morning. We will be competing in the dessert round of the competition. Momma is wishing me good luck when Daddy comes through the kitchen on his way out the back door to work.

Daddy says, "Good luck, Lil' Bit. You're going to be fantastic!"

"I hope so," I say. "This time Nanny and I are going to be on live TV. We are both as nervous as catfish in a hot skillet!"

Momma, T.J., and Ugly Brother are going to be watching us at home from the living room couch. Momma is going to record *Good Morning, Texas* so Daddy can watch us on TV when he gets home.

Nanny comes in as Daddy is leaving, and we all walk out together. It's a short drive to the TV station. At the studio, we sign in again with Miss Mabel. Colton and his dad are right behind us.

Mabel says, "You will be cooking in a different part of the studio this time."

Today we are on the actual set of *Good Morning, Texas*. This time everything looks the same, except there are only two work spaces.

There is also a big ice-cream maker. Across from us is another stage that has big chairs and a coffee table for the hosts of the morning program and the judges.

The hosts and the judges come over to introduce themselves. Joe Conrad is quiet, Kathy Lane is tall, and Amy Roberts is wearing a beautiful scarf. They all welcome us to the show. The camera crew waves and smiles. They all seem really nice.

Amber, the producer, explains the rules again. "This time, you have one hour to make your dessert course. Our hosts will introduce you, and then you can begin cooking."

I turn to Nanny and whisper, "There are a lot of really bright lights."

"Stay focused!" she says. "Once you start cooking, you won't even notice."

I try to think about Ugly Brother eating that bacon. It makes me smile.

One of the hosts, Vickie Baker, walks over as the show starts. She explains the contest again and welcomes us to the program. Then she asks each of us to introduce ourselves and our sous chefs. I go first.

"Good morning, Texas!" I say. "My name is Kylie Jean Carter, and I'm pleased as punch to be cooking for the judges today. This is Nanny, the best cook in Texas. If we win, we are giving all of our prize money to the Harvest Food Pantry. They feed hungry families."

Nanny looks surprised.

"Oh, and one more thing," I add. "They are taking bags of groceries. Just drop your bag off at their place downtown. Thank you for caring and for sharing!"

"That's very inspirational, Kylie Jean," Vickie Baker says. "Thank you, and good luck."

Next is Colton's introduction. "I'm Colton, and I love to cook!" he says. "This is my dad, and he is the best cook in the world."

"Good luck, Colton!" Vickie replies. "You two are already very competitive! Let's get started. Ready? Start cooking in three, two, one . . . go!"

Colton and I race to the ingredients table. I'm making my famous pecan pie because Aunt Susie told me it's a winner! I grab the pecans while Nanny goes to the refrigerator for butter and eggs. In the pantry, I grab sugar, vanilla, flour, salt, and corn syrup.

I also look for one more secret ingredient. I am thinking about what Nanny said about making my recipe special. I want to put chocolate in my pie. I look for baking chocolate bars, but Colton already took them.

Oh, no! A plain old pecan pie can never win this contest. Back at my station, I explain the situation to Nanny.

"Maybe he won't need all of the chocolate," she says. "Why don't you ask if you can have some?"

I head over to Colton's station. He is cooking something on top of the stove. I have to hurry, because my pie needs thirty minutes to bake.

"Can I please have some chocolate?" I ask.

Colton stops stirring the pot and says, "No, I'm sorry, but I'll need all of it for my ice cream."

I run back to my station and tell Nanny.

Nanny says, "We'll just do our best."

She turns on the oven while I make the piecrust, rolling it out with a big wooden rolling pin. Nanny puts the crust in the pie pan while I mix the filling. The whole time, I've been thinking about how I can make this dessert special.

Finally my pie is ready to go into the oven.

Nanny says, "Well, it looks beautiful. Let the chips fall where they may."

"Nanny, that's it!" I shout. "We can use chocolate chips instead of baking chocolate." I rush to the ingredients table and grab a bag.

When Nanny sees me sprinkle those chocolate chips all over the top of my pie, she winks at me. My pie will not be a plain old pecan pie. It will be special! We get it into the oven so it can bake.

We catch our breath for a minute. Then I realize Colton is making brownies with chocolate ice cream. It's a bake off! I decide that while my pie is in the oven, I'll make some homemade whipped cream since Colton is making ice cream!

The pie and brownies come out of the oven at almost the same time. I overhear the hosts saying they smell something delicious.

Colton and I both get our plates ready for the judges to taste. I slice my pie into a perfect wedge. Then I scoop a huge dollop of the whipped cream on top. It still looks a little plain, so I sprinkle some chocolate chips on top.

Stepping back to give my plate a final look, I think it is pretty fancy. It's perfect!

The judges taste the desserts. I watch their faces, but they seem to like both of our desserts. Vickie steps toward us with the microphone.

"Kylie Jean, can you tell us why you think you should win today?" she asks.

I turn to her and the camera. "I have a lot of experience!" I say. "My family is full of great cooks, and they've taught me everything they know. I think I should win because I put a lot of love and creativity into my food."

"Excellent!" she replies. "Colton, how about you?"

"I should win because I'm just the better cook," Colton says. "After all, I've had a professional chef as a teacher."

"Let's take a commercial break," Vickie announces. "When we return, we'll announce the winner of the *Good Morning, Texas* Kids Cooking Contest!"

The break only lasts a few minutes, but it feels like forever. The judges are still talking together, and soon the camera lights come back on. The show is starting again.

Vickie looks into the camera and says, "It was a very close contest. Both of our contestants should be so proud. Both desserts were absolutely delicious!"

Then Vickie Baker smiles and says, "In fact, they were so delicious the judges couldn't choose. We are calling the contest a tie!"

Nanny and I are surprised. We laugh and hug.

"You two will have to share the prize money," Vickie says. "Each of you will get fifty dollars."

Nanny and I walk right over to congratulate Colton and his dad. Vickie walks over too.

Colton shakes my hand. "I'd like to give you my money for the Harvest Food Pantry," he says.

"That's the nicest thing I've heard in a long time," Vickie says. "Kylie Jean wins, Colton wins, and the really big winner is the Harvest Food Pantry. If Kylie Jean and Colton can donate their winnings, I think the station can match their donations. Let's make it two hundred dollars for hungry families!"

Everyone in the studio cheers.

I go home with my chef coat, bragging rights as a real true cooking queen, and a full and happy heart! I can just imagine all the food we can buy for the food pantry. We might even be able to fill up the back of Daddy's pickup truck!

Chocolate Pecan Pie Filling
Serves 8

Ingredients

- 3 eggs
- ²/₃ cup white sugar
- ½ teaspoon salt
- ⅓ cup butter, melted
- 1 cup light corn syrup
- 1 cup pecan halves
- 1 ½ cups chocolate chips
- pie shell

Instructions

1. Preheat oven to 375ºF.
2. Mix all ingredients together in a bowl and pour into prepared pie shell. Bake for 40 minutes.

Chapter Nine
We Are THANKFUL

Early on Thanksgiving Day, Momma gets up before Mr. Rooster even crows. She needs to get our big ol' turkey in the oven so it can cook. All day long, she is rushing around getting the rest of the cooking done.

Now that it is almost time for the meal, more people are here to help in the kitchen. Aunt Susie is helping, Lilly is helping, and Lucy is helping too! I am mashing potatoes with a big potato masher.

Lucy is standing next to me. "That looks hard," she says. "Good thing you're a cooking queen!"

"The trick is to mash them without squishing them out of the bowl!" I tell her.

Family members poke their heads in the kitchen as they arrive. "Hi, y'all!" they say. "Happy Turkey Day, and congratulations, Kylie Jean, cooking queen!"

"Thank you very much, and I hope y'all will try my prize-winning pie," I reply. "It has chocolate, and you know chocolate makes everything taste better!"

More and more people arrive. Dinner is not ready, pots and pans are piling up, and Momma's to-do list on the refrigerator is still full.

Momma goes straight to Nanny and gives her a big ol' squeezy hug. She says, "Maybe it's not time for you to quit cooking Thanksgiving dinner after all. Just look at this mess!"

Nanny smiles and says, "I just happen to have my apron in my purse!"

Lilly leaves to help T.J. and Daddy set up extra tables in the living room. Pa comes in to help in the kitchen. With Nanny giving the orders like a head chef, the food is ready in no time!

Lucy, Daddy, Lilly, and I carry big bowls of steaming hot food out to the serving table. Everyone has finally arrived. We all find a place at the table. Daddy carves the turkey. While we pass the dishes and load our plates, everyone takes turns saying what he or she is thankful for.

Momma says, "I am grateful that my mom is going to take back that turkey platter, because cooking Thanksgiving dinner is a huge job!"

Nanny says, "I'm thankful that I have my platter back, because cooking for this family makes me very happy!"

When it's my turn, I think about all the folks down at the food pantry. I'm so glad they will have food to eat today. I may be a cooking queen, but that's not what's really important. I look up at everyone around me and say, "I am thankful for all of the delicious food we have to eat and for my wonderful family!"

Leftover Turkey Sandwiches
Serves 6–10

Ingredients

- 2 slices of your favorite bread
- 2 slices of leftover Thanksgiving turkey
- 1 tablespoon of mayonnaise
- 1 tablespoon of cranberry relish
- 2 lettuce leaves, rinsed and dried

Instructions

1. Lay the pieces of bread on a plate or cutting board.
2. Spread the mayonnaise on one slice and the cranberry relish on the other.
3. Put turkey and lettuce on the cranberry relish slice and top with the bread that has the mayonnaise on it.
4. Cut in half diagonally.

Marci Bales Peschke was born in Indiana, grew up in Florida, and now lives in Texas with her husband, two children, and a cat named Cookie. She loves reading and watching movies.

When **Tuesday Mourning** was a little girl, she knew she wanted to be an artist when she grew up. Now, she is an illustrator who lives in Utah. She especially loves illustrating books for kids and teenagers. When she isn't illustrating, Tuesday loves spending time with her husband, who is an actor, and their two sons and one daughter.

Glossary

advantage (uhd-VAN-tij)—something that helps you or puts you ahead

competitive (kuhm-PET-i-tiv)—very eager to win, succeed, or excel

crimp (krimp)—to make wavy

distract (di-STRAKT)—to draw the attention away from something

inspire (in-SPIRE)—to fill someone with an emotion, an idea, or an attitude

producer (pruh-DOOS-ur)—a person who is in charge of making a TV program

rave (RAYV)—to praise something enthusiastically

scamper (SKAM-pur)—to run lightly and quickly

setback (SET-bak)—a problem that delays you or keeps you from making progress

Talk!

1. Kylie Jean celebrates Thanksgiving with special food and special people. For what things are you thankful? Talk with a friend about all your gratitude!

2. When Kylie Jean feels nervous, she thinks of Ugly Brother cheering her on. When do you feel nervous? What could you do to feel better the next time you are nervous?

3. What would you do if you won one hundred dollars? Talk about your answer with a friend. Imagine how you could work together!

Be Creative!

1. Kylie Jean sure wanted to help hungry folks. How else could she have helped if there was no cooking competition? Make a list of three ideas, and show it to an adult. Ask if you can try out one of your ideas!

2. Plan a potluck dinner. What dish would you bring? Who could help you cook? Who would you invite? Make a guest list, and write out the ingredients you will need.

3. Draw a picture of a cool apron. Will it be your favorite color? Maybe the apron will have special pockets or a fun image on it!

This is the perfect treat for any Cooking Queen!
Just make sure to ask a grown-up for help.

Love, Kylie Jean

From Momma's Kitchen

Cheesy Macaroni with Ham

YOU NEED:

- 1 package elbow macaroni
- 1/3 cup butter
- 1/2 cup chopped onion
- 2 teaspoons minced garlic
- 2 teaspoons flour
- 3 1/2 cups warmed milk
- 4 cups grated cheddar cheese
- salt and pepper
- 2 cups cubed ham
- 2/3 cup bread crumbs
- 2 teaspoons olive oil

1. Preheat oven to 350°F.

2. Bring a large pot of water to a boil. Add pasta and cook according to package instructions. Drain.

3. Sauté onions in a pot with melted butter for 2 minutes. Add garlic and sauté for another minute. Add flour and stir constantly for 2 minutes. Add milk, stirring constantly until sauce is smooth. Bring to a boil and cook for 1 minute.

4. Remove from heat and add cheese until melted. Then add cubed ham. Season with salt and pepper.

5. Add sauce to cooked pasta. Spoon into buttered casserole dish (9 x 13).

6. Mix bread crumbs with olive oil. Sprinkle over pasta. Bake for 30 minutes.

Yum, yum!

THE FUN DOESN'T STOP HERE!

Discover more at www.capstonekids.com

- Videos & Contests
- Games & Puzzles
- Friends & Favorites
- Authors & Illustrators

Find cool websites and more books like this one at www.facthound.com. Just type in the Book ID: **9781479598991** and you're ready to go!